Katherine A Young

Stories of the Maple Land

Tales of the early days of Canada for children

Katherine A Young

Stories of the Maple Land
Tales of the early days of Canada for children

ISBN/EAN: 9783744750424

Printed in Europe, USA, Canada, Australia, Japan

Cover: Foto ©Andreas Hilbeck / pixelio.de

More available books at **www.hansebooks.com**

STORIES

OF THE

MAPLE LAND

*TALES OF THE EARLY DAYS OF CANADA
FOR CHILDREN.*

BY

KATHERINE A. YOUNG,

HAMILTON.

TORONTO:
THE COPP, CLARK, COMPANY, LIMITED.
1898.

STORIES OF THE MAPLE LAND.

THE MAPLE-TREE'S STORY.

The Maple-tree and the Horse-chestnut grew close together, just by the side of the big school. They both were very fond of the children, and might often have been seen with their branches twined together peeping through the windows.

This morning the Maple seemed in high spirits. Indeed she had just been given a new spring dress, and very proud she was of it, too. No wonder either, for it was such a dainty, fresh shade of green, and her branches looked so graceful with their weight of baby leaves, from which the sun had kissed away the last stubborn twist and wrinkle.

The Horse-chestnut felt rather dull. She was not dressed yet, and was out of sorts because the sun had not given her enough help. The spring days had been chilly, so she had not been

1

able to open her sticky buds nor prepare her clusters of snowy blossoms. And here was that tall Maple with every branch clothed and her blossoms all ready. Really, she felt quite plain and dowdy beside her.

"What's the matter?" she asked in her quiet manner. "You're making a dreadful fuss, rustling your leaves, and shaking yourself so often."

"Oh!" cried the happy Maple, "I was just trying to get up a breeze to bend me over to you. You were so busy you wouldn't look, and I wanted to tell you what I heard this morning."

"What was it?" asked the Chestnut, full of curiosity, for the Maple being tall heard much more than she did.

"Listen!" said the Maple, bending her head. And the spring breeze carried the words of the children's song out to the trees:

"The maple leaf, our emblem dear,
    The maple leaf forever.
God save our Queen, and Heaven bless,
    The maple leaf forever."

All the Maple's branches shook with delight as she heard the soft music.

"You know my pretty green leaf is the emblem of Canada," she said, turning to the Horse-chestnut. "And I've often told you how many of our family live in this country, and have lived here for hundreds of years. Indeed, I have heard my grandfather say that we had relatives in every part of the land. Our family were here when there were no white folks, only great bands of red-skinned Indians. There were more forests then, and whole hundreds of us lived together. My father used to tell me wonderful tales of those days."

"Well, you have told me all that before," said the Chestnut-tree. "Tell me what you heard to-day."

"I was coming to that," answered the Maple, who, like everybody else, wanted to tell her story in her own way. "The children were all listening to a story to-day. I wondered why they were so quiet and peeped in at them. The story sounded so much like my grandfather's stories, that I waited to hear it. It was lovely; all about the country and the people. The children liked it, and so did I. I tapped on the window to let them know how I liked it, but of course they never noticed me."

"Of course not!" said the Chestnut. "They just thought the wind was blowing your branches. But the story—what about it?"

"The story was all about their country—Canada, what a big, beautiful place it is. They heard about the great high mountains, and the wonderful forests, where nearly every kind of tree may be seen. They heard about the large lakes, the long rivers, the deep mines far down in the earth, and the rich flowers, fruits and grains.

And do you know it is really more than four hundred years ago, since a great man sailed from a country far across the seas, and found out the country we live in, for the first time. The man's name was Christopher Columbus, and he came from a place called Spain.

I don't know where that is, and I don't suppose the children do either."

"Oh, I think they do," said the quiet Chestnut. "You see they're people, and people know more than trees."

"Well, about some things," said the Maple, who thought she knew quite a lot herself.

"Then there was a good deal more about the big forests that I was used to hearing about before my Grandfather Maple died, and about the Indians whom the white people had to fight at first, before they could get a place in the land.

And now there are many millions of people living here, there are great noisy cities, long railroads which go from one end of the country to the other, and boats which sail over the great lakes, and down the rivers."

"I wish I had heard it," was the Chestnut's answer, when the Maple finished her story.

"Oh, I'm sure there is to be another story to-day. We shall watch and wait for it."

So the branches of the two trees were twined lovingly together as they peeped through the window. And this is the story they heard that bright Spring afternoon, though no one would have thought they were listening.

We like to go fast, and indeed we need to go fast, for we want to take a long journey, so we will step on a train. Of course we must sit by a window, because we want to see how quickly everything flies past us, as the puffing iron-horse carries the long train of cars behind him.

On we rush, past fields of tasselled corn and golden wheat. Out in the hot sun the busy farmers stand, hard at work, for they must gather in their summer's crop.

We pass the pretty farm-house, where the roses climb, and the yellow sunflowers and the gay hollyhocks hold up their bright heads and smile at us.

Now we see a field where the horses, cows, and sheep are busy cropping the sweet, green grass. They lift their heads lazily as we whizz past them, and gaze with wonder at us. One merry little colt takes a run with us as far as the fence of the field. Our last backward look sees him galloping wildly back to his playfellows. And we are far ahead, seeing something new.

Now it is a thick, green woods. It looks so cool and quiet, we wish the train would stop and let us get off to wander there awhile. We can almost think we see the wild flowers and the dewy ferns. And we know, too, that there we should see the merry squirrel and the saucy woodpecker, with their friends, all gay, and happy, and noisy.

But we are far past the green woods now, and the iron-horse and his load are crawling over a high bridge. Far below us we see the silver water of a river. The breeze sends a gentle little ripple over the water. A merry boat-load of children are picking yellow and white water-lilies, and shouting gaily at us as the train moves along.

Next we catch a flying glimpse of a tiny white house. A group of bare-footed children stare at us as we pass. They wave their little brown hands in greeting, and a white handkerchief floats far out of the car window in reply.

And now we reach a big, noisy city. The

train rattles into a large station. Here we see engines, and cars, and people everywhere. There is noise and confusion, men shouting and bells ringing. But it is not long till we leave the station. An electric car whirls us as quickly as the steam engine through busy streets, past tall buildings and blocks of stores bright with light. We run between rows of dark trees, past pretty houses, and silent schools and churches, till at last we reach our journey's end and are ready for supper and a long nap.

But a trip through the land of Canada was not always like the one we have just had.

We will try to think back two hundred years or more. We find ourselves in the long ago, and now we will take another journey through the same land.

Things look very strange to our eyes. What a wild looking place! We are almost afraid to trust ourselves in those thick, dark forests. They look as if they were the home of many wild creatures, and we are not very anxious to meet with wild animals.

But, of course, we have our guns with us, for we may catch our dinner in that woods.

How different everything looks! There are no roads, and if there were, we have no waggons to travel in! We cannot go by the railroad either, for there are no rails to be seen, no fine car on this trip, with windows, and cushions, and electric lights, and no strong engine to pull us along.

9

We follow a narrow, beaten track for a while, but we cannot go very far, for a long stream of water stretches across our path. But we can go on the water, for here we see a boat. Even this looks strange. It is a long, slim, odd-looking boat which we call a canoe.

Into it we step, and are surprised to feel how quickly we are carried down the silent river. The shore on each side of us is very beautiful. The wild fowl fly up in great numbers, frightened by our quiet coming. All along the banks of the river the thick, green stuffs hang heavy. Trees, and shrubs, and vines are there closely twined together, while dainty flowers, tall strong reeds, and brown bulrushes grow almost in reach of our hands, as we pass along.

There are no sights of pretty farm houses on our way. We pass through no lively city, see no tall buildings, and no church spires. But instead we see miles and miles of thick trees, great stretches of flat land, and long shining rivers.

But we can go no farther in our canoe just now, so we jump out on land. We have to carry our boat with us, however. It is very light, and we will need it when we come to water again. Through the dense forest we again follow the narrow path.

Such a thick growth we pass through! Very few trees have felt the axe in this woods. The berries hang ripe and red on the bushes beside us. Very few merry children have ever come here to pick them.

We forget to feel frightened of the animals we see, for at the first sound we make, they speed away more frightened than we are.

Everything is very beautiful, very wonderful, but very, very quiet.

It is so quiet that we really begin to feel frightened at the great stillness. Soon, however, we leave the dark woods and find ourselves standing on a little clearing, right in the midst of a crowd of strange-looking people.

It is a new and surprising sight we now see. Such fierce, dark-looking men and women are here, the like of which we have never seen before. In a flash it comes to us. We know who they are, these tall, silent, red children of the forest.   They are the Indians, and we have been travelling through the early home of the red man.

Our trip has ended at a real Indian camp. We are sure to find it interesting to watch them. So we will stay awhile with the Indian, and see how he lived so long ago.

————————

THE RED-MAN.

Here we see a group of such queer-looking houses. The Indian calls them his wigwams. They are built of the branches of trees joined together at the top. Then they are covered over with sheets of bark, which the Indians peel from the birch trees around them. Over the bark the Indian hangs curtains made of the skins of deer.

We step close up to one of these wigwams and peep inside. These are friendly Indians, so they do not mind us. Right in the middle of the floor of the wigwam we see an Indian woman building a fire. Looking up, we see the smoke rising to the sky through a real Indian chimney—only a hole at the top of the wigwam. On the ground we see the bed—not a very fine one, we think. Just a soft nest of dry pine-needles gathered in the forest. Yet the Indian sleeps very soundly here, and if the house does look poor and small to us, he and his children are very well pleased with it, and live very happily in it.

Sometimes, for company and for safety, a row of these wigwams are built, making a long narrow house called the "long-house." Then a number of Indian families live there together.

We are making this visit in summer-time, so we find most of the Indians wearing no clothes at all. If it were winter we should find them dressed in clothes made of the skins of wild animals. Round the thick forests they find plenty of bear, buffalo, and beaver. When they kill these animals they get all the material they need for clothes.

Over in one part of the camp we see a large crowd. Here are a lot of young Indians getting ready for a feast. They have painted themselves all over in bright colors. In their hair they have stuck long stiff feathers. They are making horrible faces, and dancing and singing in a very wild manner, getting ready for the good time they will have, we suppose. We do not feel very much like going to the feast with such company, so we leave them very gladly.

The Indian seems to us a very lazy man. We see so many lying around doing nothing, while the poor Indian women are doing all the hard work. Some of the women are working with clay. As we watch them, we see them make a very good pot out of the wet clay and put it in the sun to bake hard. They have to make all their own pots which they need for cooking. Some other women are cutting wood. Others are carrying water from the lake far away. Some old Indian "squaws" are cooking the dinner, and others are sitting making the clothes out of the deer skins and furs.

Some of the Indian men and boys have been out hunting. We see them coming back with only their spears and arrows. We think they have shot nothing, but in a little while some of the women come along carrying between them the animals which have been shot. The men never carry home anything they have killed. They think *that* beneath them and leave it for the women to do.

Down by the lake we come across some more Indians fishing. The hooks they are using have been cut out of bone. Some, however, have nets.

We find some here, too, making a new canoe,

or boat. Over a light wooden frame they have stretched the bark cut from the birch tree. All the cracks and seams in this canoe will soon be daubed with pitch. Then, the boat the Indian loves will be firm and water-tight.

If we could talk to the Indians standing around us, they would tell us many strange things about themselves.

If we should ask them : " Do you believe in God ? " they would say :

" Oh, yes ! The Indian believes in the Great Spirit." The Manitou, or chief spirit, they call their God.

They would tell you, too, that they think that all animals have spirits. Sometimes before they catch a fish, or bear, or fowl, they talk to them, and ask them to be good, and let themselves be caught. Then they say : " We will treat your bones well, and see that you are properly cared for."

The Indians are divided into many tribes. Each tribe has a number of families in it. Each family has a name taken from a plant or an animal. So in the camp we hear of the Wolf family, the Cat family, and the Turtle family. Each tribe has its own doctor, or "medicine-man," as they call him. This "medicine-man" is held to be very wise. He cures all the sick people, and also tells of things that are going to happen. The Indian believes firmly all he says, and is in great fear of the "medicine-man."

The tribes are always fighting with each other. They use arrows, spears, and axes called toma-hawks to fight with. The Indians are cunning fighters, and often are very cruel when they take a prisoner. They torture him, as they call it, and take great joy in it. Sometimes the really savage tribes kill and eat their prisoner. After killing an enemy they take off his scalp, that is the skin of his head, with their tomahawks. They carry this home as a prize, strung around their waists.

The more scalps an Indian carries home to his village, the greater man he becomes.

That is the Indian of long ago. The Indian of to-day does not look much like him. The Red-man, like the country, has changed his looks a good deal in two hundred years.

2

The Indian camp we have just left is nowhere to be found to-day. Some Indians come to our cities from the Indian reserves round about us.

But they do not come in war-paint and feathers. Nor do they bring long strings of purple and white beads, "wampum" they called it, to use for money. Now they wear clothes like ours, and use money made of silver and paper, the same as we do.

But for many years they lived just as we have now seen them. They did not know nor care about the white people living in the other half of the world.

But one day the white man came and the Indian's free, happy, life was over.

Once he had roamed over the whole land, now he has to live in a small part of it.

Once the Indian owned everything—now the white man owns it all.

Once the land had been his happy hunting-ground, now in many places it is strange and unknown to the Red-man.

But it took a long time to change all this.

Many fierce wars were fought before the wild savages were tamed, and made willing to live as the white man lived.

We have many traces of the Indians left to us. Some of our largest cities, and rivers, and lakes still bear Indian names.

Even the name of our country, Canada, came first of all from an Indian name Kanata, which means "a group of huts."

As we have found out so much about the Red-man, we will now want to hear how the white man first found Canada, and how he made a home there for himself.

THE FIRST WHITE MEN.

"That was a fine story about the Indian camp. I wish we were going to hear some more of it."

It was the voice of the Horse-chestnut whispering softly to the Maple.

"Oh! I've heard so much about the Indians I'm a little tired of them," said the lofty Maple, shaking her branches very proudly.

"I'm glad we are soon going to hear about the white men," she went on. "They think more about us trees than the red men did. The white men plant us on their streets, water our roots carefully, trim our branches, and take great pride in us. But what did the red men do? Why, they cut our young saplings down to help build their homes whenever they felt like it, and peeled our bark off, too. They killed us, or spoiled our beauty, without thinking or caring anything about it."

"Well!" said the Chestnut, "I suppose there were so many of you, they had to do something to keep you down, or you would have taken up

all the land. You may say what you like, but I
wish I had lived in the woods of Canada then."

"Well, I would far rather live on the streets
of the city now," laughed the Maple.

"Do you think the Indians would have cared
anything about your snowy blossoms and their
dainty blush you talk so much about?"

The Chestnut looked proudly down on the soft
green tufts she was so tenderly caring for, and
shielding with her thick leaves.

"They couldn't help it," she whispered softly
to herself, but she did not say so to the Maple,
for she was afraid that lady would laugh at her.
Anyway, the story they had been waiting to hear
for some days was just started, and they must
not lose one word. They could finish their talk
again.

Our country is still called the New World. For many years the people living in the oldest parts of the world did not know anything about that part of the world where we live.

Because great seas stretched out for miles from the shores of their land, they thought that all the rest of the world was water.

But after the brave sailor from Spain, Christopher Columbus, had found a path across the unknown ocean, others soon followed.

Now right across that wide ocean, just opposite to our country, there is a country in the Old World called France. Of course, the King of France soon heard that land had been found across the sea, and thought he might as well try to get some of that great new land for France.

In one of the little seaport towns of France, where there were many sailors, men who loved the sea and did not fear its wildest storms, lived Jacques Cartier. Now Jacques was a brave, strong sailor who could sail rough seas and loved adventure. He was willing to be the King's messenger and sail to the new land. With several boats from the King, and a number of sailors like himself to sail these boats, he started across the broad, unknown Atlantic Ocean, which stretched between his sunny land lying to the south, and our colder country lying towards the north. His orders were to discover all the land he could and take it in the name of the King of France.

Jacques Cartier made at least three visits to Canada. Crossing the seas was not very easy in those days, and we may be sure Cartier and his men were very glad to sight the land, even if it was the coldest, barest spot in Canada. For the first land they touched was the rocky shore of Labrador.

From their ships, as they rowed along close to the shore, they could see people moving about on the land, or shooting past them in long, strange-looking boats. Before the Frenchmen left their ships they tried to make friends with these Indian savages who gathered around them. At first the red men were shy, and rather afraid of these strangely-dressed "pale-faces" who talked so strange and came to their land in such odd boats. But as the sailors were very kind to them, and gave them presents,—hatchets, knives, beads, and toys—the Indians soon became friendly.

And when at last Cartier landed at a point along the coast where there was a huge split rock, the Indians received him quite gladly. And when he set up a large wooden cross with three fleur-de-lis on it, and the words "Long live the King of France," the Indians did not seem to mind.

Of course they did not know what he meant by doing this. They thought he was putting up the cross to his "great spirit," and never dreamt he was, by this act, taking their land from them and handing it over to the King of France. Yet that was what he had done, for that cross standing there was to show all nations that France was the first country of the Old World to plant its banner in the New.

But the simple Indians said "Good-bye" to the French ships and the French sailors in a very friendly way, giving them their furs and fish, and getting the treasures they prized in return. The old chief of the tribe even let his two sons go away on the French ships, dressed in clothes like the Frenchmen.

When Cartier made his second trip to Canada, he took with him more ships and more men. This time he stayed longer, and saw much more of the country and the people. It was on this trip that he found out Canada's great river, the St. Lawrence.

On the feast day of St. Laurent, one of the saints which Frenchmen honor, Cartier and his men entered the little bay at the mouth of the river. In honor of the day, Cartier called it St. Laurent Bay, and afterwards the whole river and gulf took the name which it bears to this day, to tell of the first fleet of ships which floated on its waters.

The two Indians who had gone to France with Cartier, had come back with them on this trip to show them the way. So following the course of the great St. Lawrence, the French ships sailed slowly on.

They could see the Indians watching them

from the shore, but now they knew how to treat them. A few little presents always brought the Indian canoes crowding round them, loaded with Indian corn, fruit and fish. They were quite willing to trade these with the Frenchmen for beads or hatchets, or other things which pleased them.

Once, as they neared an Indian village, the chief of the tribe came out in state to visit Cartier. He had twelve canoes filled with Indians, in war-paint and feathers, with toma-hawks, and bows, and arrows. They wanted to know if the "pale-faces" had come for peace or war. Cartier took the chief into his cabin and by many signs showed him that he was kind and friendly.

Donnacona, the chief, then kissed Cartier's arm and put it round his own neck—the Indian's way of showing how friendly he was to the Frenchmen.

When Cartier's boats reached the Indian vil-lage, the Frenchmen landed, and were welcomed with joy by the Indians. They crowded round them, yelling and screeching, the squaws dancing in the water and singing them their wild Indian songs.

This little village lay at the foot of some great rocky cliffs. *Then*, those great rock hills looked down on Stadacona, a little cluster of wigwams. *Now*, those same rocks frown on the mighty city of Quebec, one of Canada's most interesting spots.

But the Indians here told Cartier of another larger Indian village farther up the river, and Cartier was anxious to go there, too. The Indians at Stadacona did not wish him to go, and tried to frighten him by telling him of dangers he would meet on the way. The Frenchman only laughed at them, and, taking his ship, sailed on.

And now the French sailors were to see sights that would repay them for all the trouble they had had on their journey. It was the fall of the year, and Canada the fair had put on her most brilliant dress. The banks of the river hung thick with vines and trees, whose green leaves had been changed to crimson, purple, and gold. Among the leaves they caught glimpses of bright colored birds, and as they sailed silently on they heard their cheery songs.

If they came near to the shore, great flocks of wild fowl rose like a cloud round their ships. They could see on the shore the wild vines hanging heavy with grapes.

Coming slowly near to an island in the river, they saw rising ahead of them a beautiful hill-slope crowned with trees.

Below it lay the village they were seeking, the great Indian town of Hochelaga.

As they landed they were met by an Indian chief and his band of braves.

Around a fire, which was very welcome in the cool fall air, all seated themselves.

The chief then spoke to them in his Indian tongue, and afterwards took from them the usual gifts of hatchets, knives, and beads. All night long, after Cartier had gone back to his boat, the savages on shore kept up their noisy welcome, dancing, and singing, and shouting.

Here Cartier had a rather strange task before him. The Indians seemed to think he could cure their diseases by touching them. So the sick, the lame, and the blind people crowded around him to get this healing touch. The French sailor hardly knew what to do, but he read to them a part of the Bible, made the sign of the cross over them, and said a short prayer. Then when he had given them a present they went off pleased.

Before Cartier left this village he climbed the mountain. He was so pleased and delighted with it, that he named it Mont Royal, or Royal Mountain, from which we now have the name Montreal.

At the foot of that mountain now stands the largest, finest city of the Dominion of Canada. It first got its name when Cartier, pleased with its beauty, planted the cross of France and sailed back to Stadacona.

But the Frenchmen found it hard to bear the long, cold Canadian winter which now followed. Before spring twenty-six of the sailors had died from the cold and disease. Cartier sailed for home when winter had gone, and it was five years before he made his third trip to Canada.

This time he found unfriendly Indians waiting

for him. When he had gone back to France the the last time he had taken with him the chief Donnacona and some of his braves, to let the people of France see how much power he had got in the new land.

Donnacona and the other Indians did not want to go, and felt very homesick and unhappy. Away from their free, wild life they died, and Cartier had to go back without them.

The Indians of Canada came crowding out to him as usual when his ships came up the river. They wanted news of their friends, and Cartier, afraid to tell them the truth, told them lies which the Indians were wise enough not to believe.

This winter was worse than the last to Cartier and his men, for they were not only sick, half-frozen and unhappy, but they were afraid to trust the Indians living all around them.

When spring came, Cartier was glad enough to get back to France, without finding out much more of the country. It is not likely that he ever saw Canada again, for he settled down in his old home in France.

But Jacques Cartier had done a great deal. He was the first man to open up our great beautiful country, and Canadian boys and girls all have cause to remember the brave French sailor, Jacques Cartier.

———————

THE FRENCH GIRL ON THE LONELY ISLAND.

No one has ever heard or read of all the strange adventures which happened to the first white settlers of Canada.

Many of those people who left France for the New World never went back to tell of their wonderful wild life in the new land. Most of them died out in Canada far from home, and found a lonely grave in the dark forests, or beneath the stormy waters of the ocean.

For those early days were full of trouble and danger to all. . Not many of us would care to leave our comfortable, happy, homes, sail far over a stormy sea, and land in an unknown country, with no house to live in, and no friends to gather around us, but savage Indians or wild beasts.

It is little wonder then, that those who did come, went gladly back the first chance they had.

But there is one story told of these early days which many of us would like to hear, because it tells us what it really was like to live in our country in the early days.

The story is about a young, French girl who bore the very pretty name of Marguerite de Roberval.

Marguerite's uncle was a Frenchman, who had got leave from the King to go to the new world to try to start a French colony there, in that wonderful country which Cartier had found. To do this he took with him a number of people in his ships, who were willing to live in Canada, as they thought. And being very fond of his gay, bright, happy little niece, he took her too. Marguerite was a great favorite, and was loved by all her uncle's friends.

But alas! before the new land was reached Marguerite had done wrong and disobeyed her uncle. And while he loved her, yet he was hard and stern, and said she must be punished for her wrong-doing.

They were nearing Canada now, and as they began to see the shores of Newfoundland, they passed close by a lonely island.

When sailors pass that dark spot, they look

3

upon it with great fear, and tell wild stories of evil spirits living upon it. Even above the roar of the waters they say, they can hear groans and cries coming from the rocky spot.

The ship of stern Captain Roberval stopped here. Poor Marguerite, with a cry for mercy, begged her hard uncle not to punish her in such a terrible way.

But all in vain, for here she was left, with her old nurse for company, at the mercy of the cruel winds and savage beasts, while her uncle's ship passed slowly on.

But one on that ship could not bear to leave sweet Marguerite to such a lonely fate. As the ship sailed off, her young lover cast himself into the sea, and being able to swim well, soon reached her on the shore. For a long while this little band of three stood there, watching the white sails of the ship till they faded out of sight. They hoped and hoped that the uncle would feel sorry, think he had punished them enough, and return for them. But even this hope died out as days and weeks passed by without a sign of the returning sails.

There was nothing for them to do but to make the best of their hard lot.

Out of the boughs of the trees they built themselves a rude, little hut.

They had some guns, so found plenty of work to do, shooting wild fowl, bears and other animals.

By this means they got food and skins out of which they could make clothes, for the wild, stormy winter would soon be upon them.

And the dark days passed on, lonely days indeed, for there was no company but the trees and rocks, and wandering animals. At night they heard strange music, as they sat in their little hut, but it was only the wail of the winds, the dash of the waters, or the roar of the wild beasts.

There amid the still quiet of their island home, during the cold winter days, a little child was sent from Heaven to brighten the lives of the lonely family.

But alas! it did not take kindly to the cold, cruel, winter winds, and stayed but a short time to cheer its young mother.

Poor Marguerite, it is hard to tell how she lived through the long, dreary days, for it was not long before Death broke up the little family circle and left her alone.

There on the island for nearly two years she lived by herself, praying often that God would take her too, to His bright home.

Many an hour she sat watching the restless, moving sea. Beyond that sea lay France, her sunny home-land. How she longed to see it once more. And with her hand to her head she strained her eyes to see, if by any chance, a vessel's sail was in sight.

One day her watching eye saw the wished-for sail. Oh! that they might see her! How far away they seemed!

With great care she gathered together the twigs and grass and dry branches, and before long the flames of a huge bonfire flamed up to the sky. The smoke was seen by the sailors.

At first they were afraid when they saw the smoke coming from the much-feared island of demons. But by-and-bye they came nearer.

They were able to see a woman in her strange dress of skins making signs to them.

The rough sailors had only to hear Marguerite's sad story, in order to pity her, and want to help her. Very soon she was on the sea, bound for France. Kind friends welcomed her back, more than ready to make up to her for all she had suffered.

So long as she lived, we are sure Marguerite never forgot those three years of her life in wild Canada. Many a strange tale she would have to tell. But none of them have been left to us, and except her name we know very little of Marguerite, who spent three years alone in Canada.

SAMUEL DE CHAMPLAIN AND THE INDIANS.

One of the best known and best loved Frenchmen who came to Canada in those early days, was Samuel Champlain.

In those days he won the name of "the father of New France," and what he did for young Canada has been told in many ways. Even yet, we hear echoes of his deeds and his name. In Lower Canada we find a beautiful lake bearing his name, because he first found it out; and there, too, is pointed out Champlain street and Champlain market, spots where in early days the great Frenchman had his home.

Champlain was an explorer. That is, he was a man who dearly loved to wander over all parts of the country, and find out all about it. He was a brave soldier, and very fond of adventures. When he came to the new country he wanted to travel over all the great lakes and rivers, and try to find a path through the new world which would lead him into the old world.

But there was another great thing he hoped to
do.   He had a great love and pity for the poor
red men, whose lives seemed to him to be so
unhappy.   They did not believe in his God, for
one thing, and when he came to live amongst
them he hoped to be able to make them good
men and lovers of the true God.

But he soon found that work among the
Indians was very hard work.

To begin with, all the red men living in wigwams were not good friends.   We saw before
that the different tribes were always fighting
with each other.   Now the strongest of these
tribes, the ones which had the most power, were
the Iroquois, or Five Nations.

These were very brave, fierce Indians, and
they were always ready for war.   They never
spared any one, but rushed on their enemies with
raised tomahawks, ready to do their worst.

The other tribes of Indians, mostly those called
Hurons and Algonquins, were in great fear of
these savage Iroquois, who showed neither pity
nor fear.

When Champlain came to Canada to build

up homes for all who cared to live in the new land, he tried at once to find the Indian villages which Cartier had visited.

But not a trace of Stadacona or Hochelaga could be seen. They had all been burned and ruined by the wars of the Iroquois.

Quite near to where the village of Stadacona had been, Champlain tried to start a new village. The place he picked out to build his fort was called by the Indians living around it "Kebec," meaning "a narrow place." Just at this point the great river St. Lawrence does become narrow, so the new village got its name Quebec.

Here Champlain set his men to clear away the thick trees and build a fort. This he called his home; here he made himself a garden, with flowers and vegetables in it, and here, some time afterwards, he brought his wife, Helen Champlain.

For four or five years this kind, gentle lady from France lived in wild, stormy Canada. We remember her now by the name of an island near Montreal, called Helen's Isle, after the wife of Champlain.

She was very good, and brave, too, and won the hearts of the rough Indians. She loved to teach the squaws and their children.

The Indians round there were friendly to Champlain, and were very pleased with the lovely, white lady, his wife.

Like other French ladies of her time, she always carried a little mirror hung at her waist. The Indians would crowd round her, peering into it, to see their own faces. Then they said to each other that the white lady must love them very much, for she carried their pictures so close to her all the time.

The Huron and Algonquin Indians came to trust Champlain very much. They felt that he was their friend, and they asked him to visit their part of the country. They were quite willing that he should build a fort and teach them about his God, if he would only help them to fight the hated Iroquois.

This he promised to do, and went with them long journeys through the land, searching and ever finding something that made him love the

great, new land better than ever. On one of
these journeys he first saw the beautiful stretch
of water, Lake Champlain. Not far from it lay
the bark wigwam villages of the Iroquois. And
here Champlain helped his Indian friends to
fight the Iroquois. But oh! how he hated to
see them torture the prisoners which they gained
in the battle. He begged of them to set them
free, but they were too fond of their cruel tricks
to do that, even for the "man of the iron breast,"
as they called Champlain.

Champlain had very hard times on his journeys
with the Indians. They would not help him to
explore the country at all. One time he had to
spend a whole winter with them in the heart of
the forest, for they would not take him home as
they had promised.

He used to go with them hunting and fishing,
and once he lost himself, and was in the forest
all alone for days and nights without shelter.
He went with them, too, on their long marches
through mud and slush, or on snow-shoes through
the deep snow.

He had been away about a year before he got

back to his little home at Quebec.   By this time he had gone farther into the country than any other white man had ever been before.   He had found out a good deal about the land, which he took care to tell to those at home in France. Now he thought to stay at home in Quebec and do good there.

At the foot of the beautiful mountain Cartier had liked so much, Mount Royal, he picked out a spot for another town.   Here he could- trade with the Indians, for they gladly brought their furs and skins to him.   They trusted him, but not the other greedy fur traders, who were always cheating them.   So Montreal was started by the "father of New France."

While Champlain was in Canada, the first missionaries or preachers came to Canada from France.   They were Jesuit priests, and they came to help Champlain to teach Christ's mes- sage to the poor red man.   We shall soon see how they too, won the Indian hearts to love them by their kind words and deeds.   But the brave, kind leader, Champlain, did not stay much longer with his much-loved people in his well-loved land. When he died and left his two small towns, with no one to care for them, all Canada felt sorrow for the loss of one who had tried to do so much for her.

THE MISSIONARIES AND THE INDIANS.

"What is a missionary, anyway?" asked the Horse-chestnut of the Maple. "I never heard of one before."

"Oh, I don't think we have them in Canada now," replied the Maple. "But I believe they send them away to other countries. A missionary is a person who teaches about the Bible."

"Well, then, we have lots of them here," said the Chestnut.

"No, we haven't. What do we need missionaries for? Look at all the churches you can see, just as we stand here."

"But you said, a missionary taught about the Bible, and isn't that what they do in the big churches?"

"Well, it isn't in the same way. They do not call them missionaries when they do their teaching in churches." The Maple was not quite sure herself, but then she did not want to let the Chestnut know that.

"Then a missionary never has a church? Does he do all his teaching outside?"

Really, that Chestnut was troublesome, asking so many questions.

"How should I know?" the Maple said quite crossly. "I never saw one. Anyway, if you will wait and listen, you will soon hear all about what they used to do in Canada. And I suppose what they did here then, they do in other countries now. For I have heard that they do send men and women from Canada now, away to the other part of the world, to India and China, to teach about the Bible."

So the Chestnut had to be content with this, and wait patiently till she heard the story of the first missionaries in Canada. As soon as a new country is discovered by the daring explorers, and settled by the brave people who are willing to risk their lives in the new land, they are always followed by good men and women with the Bible, anxious to tell of God, and of His love for all men.

This is what happened in young Canada's early days. Side by side with brave soldiers and eager explorers like Champlain, went the black-robed priests, the Jesuit missionaries. They, in turn, were followed by good, brave women, also anxious to teach the gospel and care for the sick and the poor ones.

These men and women cared little for the riches of the country ; they did not care to see how big it was, nor to see how many towns they could build up, nor how many fur-skins they could take from the Indians.

But they did want to show the Indians their true God, and build up firmly their church in the new land.

So from old France came many brave men and women to the new world.

For weary months and long years they lived among the Indians, working for them, praying for them, loving them, and trying to win their love in return.

We should think that the Indians would be only too glad to return their kindness in giving up so much to work for them.

But instead of that, the Indians very often

hated them, said evil things against them, and
even put some of them to death.

The first missionary to Canada was Paul Le
Jeune. He came to Canada while Champlain
was still living. He kept a book in which he
wrote down all that happened to him in his
work among the savages. When he first saw
the Indians he thought them a very queer-
looking people. He was sitting in the cabin of
the ship in which he had crossed the ocean,
when suddenly in walked ten or twelve Indians.
They were a fearful sight to the eyes of the
Frenchman.

Some had their cheeks painted black, their
noses blue, and the rest of their faces red.
Others had a broad band of black across their
eyes, and others had tried to make themselves
look like a rainbow. For clothes they wore old,
shaggy bear-skins.

The missionary began his work with a small
school of two pupils, one a little Indian boy, the
other a negro, and not one of the three could tell
what the other was saying.

Le Jeune was very anxious to learn to speak

Indian, and tried in every way to learn the language.

One time he came across a band of Indians who were fishing for eels on the St. Lawrence River. A little boy asked him into his grandmother's house, which was a bark wigwam, of course, where many eels were strung up to dry.

The missionary was given some smoked eels on a piece of birch bark. The squaws sat round toasting their eels on a stick over the fire. Then, when all was ready, the feast began. It was neither very clean nor nice for the missionary to see the Indians wipe their fingers on their hair, or on that of their dogs. He tried to talk with them, but he found it very slow work.

At last, however, he got Pierre, a young Indian who knew both French and Indian, to come and live with him and be his teacher.

In the little mission house they had built on the St. Lawrence River, the priest and the Indian sat together on wooden stools round a rough table. Pierre was not a very kind nor a very nice friend, and the missionary had to keep

4

coaxing him by little presents of tobacco to make him work.

But all winter they kept at it. The snow lay deep all around them, and the Indians had great fun teaching the priests to walk on snow-shoes. How they laughed at their many slips and falls in the deep drifts of snow.

Soon, however, the weather grew warm, and the soft days of spring drew near. The Indians gathered around Quebec in large crowds. The missionary used to take his stand at the door and ring a bell. This gathered a crowd of children who came running round him. Then he would teach them to pray, and to sing hymns. When school was over he gave each of the children a dish of peas to coax them to come back at his next bell-ringing.

In the fall of the year the Indians always started out on a hunting trip. When the missionary heard of this he thought he would join them. He thought by going to live right with them, he would learn so much about their ways, and might be able to do them some good.

There were about twenty in the party, men,

women and children. Pierre was one of the
party and his two brothers, one a great hunter,
who was good to the missionary. The other
was a wicked medicine-man who hated the missionary and did him all the harm he could.

For five long months they were all away.
When winter came they tramped through thick
forests, piled high with snow, across frozen lakes
and ponds, carrying great loads on their backs
and on their sledges. These were their kettles,
axes, and big rolls of birch bark for covering
their wigwams.

When they stopped to camp, these loads were
thrown down. The squaws cut long poles of
birch and spruce saplings, or young trees, while
the men cleared a big space in the snow where
they could build their wigwam.

To cover the boughs with bark, to hang a bear-
skin up for a door, to cover the ground inside
with the green spruce branches, did not take
long—and behold their home was ready.

Into this hut they all crowded—men, women,
children, and dogs—and lived there as long as
they chose to stay at that spot.

It was neither very warm nor very pleasant. The cracks in the bark covering let in the snow and bitter winds. The priest says himself that as he lay on his bed of spruce boughs he could watch the stars in the sky above, through the hole at the top of the wigwam.

Sometimes, indeed, the missionary got very tired of the dirt, the heat, the smoke, and the unkind talk of the Indians. Then he would go out into the deep forest, and there, with the snow piled high around him, and the frost gems sparkling on the trees, he read his evening prayers by the light of the moon.

The Indians stayed in one place only so long as any game was to be found there; then they moved their tent again.

Sometimes they would hunt for days and catch little or nothing. They were always very cross when they had to come back empty-handed. Some of them even blamed the missionary for bringing them bad luck. At these times they would live for days on the bark of trees or bits of leather. As long as the tobacco lasted they were happy, though, because they could always smoke, and this partly satisfied their hunger.

When the milder days of April melted the snow, and warmed the air, they turned their steps towards home again. The missionary felt rather sad. He was ill and unhappy. Coming home he had nearly lost his life on the water, and it seemed as if his long months' troubles had been for nothing. The Indians did not seem to love him or his God any better than before.

But his friends in the mission house were filled with joy to see him again, and gave him a warm welcome. Champlain himself was glad to see him back, for many of them had feared that the Indians might put him to death.

So for a while the missionaries rested content in their home, doing what they could with the Indians who came to Quebec with their skins and furs to trade.

But Paul le Jeune had not given up his wish to help the Indians scattered over the big country, and before very long a new plan was formed. And this we will hear about as the work of the missionaries.

A very large number of Huron Indians lived away to the west, on the shores of the lake which to this day bears their name—Lake Huron.

A party of these Indians came down to Quebec and round about there to trade. When they went back to their home, Champlain got them to take with them three missionaries. It was a long, weary journey, nine hundred miles, and it was nearly a month before "the fathers" reached the forest shores of the blue Huron Lake.

They were weary and worn out with their long, rough journey, and half-dead from the cruel treatment they had received from some of their Indian guides.

But they were well received by the Indians there, and before very long a mission-house was built in one of the Huron towns.

It was built very much like the Indian wig-wams. A frame-work of strong sapling poles was first made, and covered over with sheets of bark.

Inside it was divided into three rooms, each of which had a wooden door—a wonderful thing in the eyes of the Indians. The first room was a sort of hall and store-room in one. The second and largest room was kitchen, dining-room, workshop, school-room and bed-room. Their fire was on the ground in this room.

The third room was the church or chapel. Here they said their prayers, here they had their images, and here hung their pictures.

The missionaries had plenty of visitors. The Indians were all very anxious to see inside the house of the "black-robes," as they called the priests.

One of the greatest sights, to them, was the clock. They called it the "Captain." They thought it was alive and asked the priests what it ate. They would sit around very quietly waiting for it to strike. As the last stroke sounded one of the Frenchmen would cry "stop!" To the Indians' surprise the clock at once stopped, as they thought because the Frenchman told it to do so.

"What does 'Captain' say?" they would ask.

"When he strikes twelve he says, 'Hang on the kettle,' and when he strikes four he says, 'Get up and go home!'" was the answer.

They used to remember these words. While they were always ready to stay to dinner, they always walked quietly out when "Captain" struck four. And the missionaries would be left in peace to read and study for a while.

They liked to look at the Frenchmen's tools, were always anxious to turn the wheel of the little hand-mill, or to look at a tiny insect through the glass which made it look such a fierce monster.

The missionaries tried very hard to learn to speak like the Indians, and never lost a chance to do them good. The Indians came to trust them very much, and chiefs of other villages often came to ask them to live in their village. At one time the missionaries had eleven mission houses in the Huron district and priests working in all of them.

But through it all they had many trials. At one time they were blamed because the small-pox had come into the Indian camps and made

many die. Another time the red cross in front
of their house was said to be keeping the rain
and thunder away during a long spell of dry
weather.

Yet the missionaries were very good to the
Indians. If any one was suffering they were
always on hand to help. They gathered the
children around them wherever they went, and
taught them little prayers which they had made
to fit some of the Indian songs. And the children were well enough pleased to come, for they
never went away without some little present,
two or three beads perhaps, or some raisins.

The Indians were very slow to believe all " the
fathers " told them of Heaven.

" It is good for the French, not so good for the
Indians. Indian man is different to white man,
and has different ways." This was always their
ready answer.

" Heaven is a good place for Frenchmen, but
I want to be among Indians, for the French will
give me nothing to eat when I get there."

" Do they hunt in Heaven, or make war, or go
to feasts ? " asked another.

"Oh, no!" said the missionary.

"Then I will not go," said the Indian. "It is not good to be lazy."

Sometimes when they sat teaching the Indians who liked them, other rude ones would gather round and annoy them. Suddenly a shower of sticks, snowballs or corncobs would be thrown in on them through the window.

The Indians would hardly let them baptize their children. "The fathers" believed this was right, and used to try to do it whenever they could. But they had to use tricks. They would make believe they were giving the child sugared water, and drop some on the child's forehead. Then saying a prayer quickly to themselves and making the sign of the cross, it was done, and the little child made fit for Heaven, as they believed.

Father Jogues, a very brave missionary, once baptized a dying Indian with a few drops of dew which he found on a cob of corn handed to him by another Indian.

But hard as they worked, and much as they tried, everything seemed to fail. The fierce

Iroquois came down amongst their mission-houses and drove the priests away. One after another of the brave missionaries met an awful death from the Indians. Jogues was asked to come to one of their feasts. But as he came into the hut he was knocked on the head with a tomahawk. Brebeuf, another brave Jesuit, was tied to a stake and cruelly treated. A necklace of red-hot tomahawks was thrown around his neck. But nothing they did to him made him cry or groan. He was as brave as a lion, and when he was dying the Indians came in a crowd to drink his blood. They hoped to get some of his courage by doing this.

Down in a large church at Quebec the skull of this brave man lies in a silver case, carefully kept to this very day.

But after all their toil and trouble very little is now left to show how much the missionaries worked and suffered in the early days of Canada.

"Now you know what a missionary is," said the Maple.

"Yes," replied the Chestnut, giving such a

deep sigh that all her leaves rustled, and her clusters of blossoms waved restlessly.

"But they had such a hard time; I feel sorry for them. I hope they don't have such hard times now."

"Oh, everybody had a hard time then; I think everything is much better now," was the Maple's cheerful reply. But the Chestnut was very quiet. School was out, and the boys were trying very hard to rob her of her treasured flowers. She did want to keep some, for what would the boys think in the fall if she had no nuts for them? So she did her best to keep some prize ones just beyond their reach. It was hard work, though, and she could not quite agree with the Maple's cheerful words.

THE FRENCH GARDENS OF ACADIA.

Down hear the coast of Nova Scotia there is a little, bare, lonely island. It is only a strip of sandy land, plain and dreary looking. But one spot on that island bears, to this day, the name French Gardens, and has its own story to tell of Canada's early days.

In those wild times a party once set sail for Canada. In this party was one ship with a strange load—forty men taken from the prisons of France, and promised their freedom if they would come to the New World.

The leader of the party landed this ship-load on the little island—called the Isle of Sable. Then he sailed away to pick out a place on the mainland, called in those days Acadia, for them to settle on. He expected to come back to the island in a short time and get the men, but somehow things went against him. A fierce wind sprang up and swept his ships back to France. There he was seized and put in prison, and there he stayed for five long years.

At first the men left on the island were quite
well pleased. After being in prison, it was quite
a change to be free and to roam about as they
wished. There was no one to watch them, or to
punish them in any way. So they took great
pleasure in wandering over the sand, shooting
the wild-duck and wild animals, and eating the
berries that grew so thickly in the sand of the
island.

Every day they expected their leader back
with the ships. But time passed on, their food
became scarce and the weather grew cold. They
had to build themselves a house. They had no
means of lighting fires, and so had to live on the
raw flesh of the animals they killed. They soon
got to like it, but eating so much raw meat made
them all the more fierce and wild. They began
to fight and even to kill each other, for there was
no one to keep them in order.

The long months now grew into years. They
did not fight much now, for their number was
getting small. Their hut they had built in the
deepest heart of the island to protect themselves
from the bitter winds that stormed around their

island prison. For warmth and for company they all gathered there close together. There were plenty of seals on the island, and these they caught and made clothes for themselves out of the skins.

The time dragged on, but the ships and the men never came for them. And now it was nearly five years since they had been left on the island. They had gathered together quite a store of sealskins, ivory from the walrus, and hides of animals. But all except twelve of the men had died.

Those who remained were strange looking indeed. They had long beards down to their waists, their skin was so hairy it looked like the fur of the animals, their nails were like birds' claws, and their eyes gleamed like those of wild beasts.

At last, news of their sad fate reached the ear of the King. He quickly sent a ship to the island to bring back all who were still there. Just as they were found on the island with long beards and claws, and shaggy coats of skin, they were taken before the King.

The King was sorry for them when he heard the story of their hardships, and gave them money, and also a free pardon so that they need not go back to prison.

Two or three of the men went back to the island again to get more furs, and for the rest of their lives followed the fur trade.

But on the still bare and lonely island there is one spot pointed out as the French Gardens—keeping in mind the trials of the poor French prisoners, sometimes called the " Forty Thieves."

A BAND OF HEROES.

"I suppose you would like to know what a 'hero' is, now," said the Maple to her friend when the name of the new story was given out.

"But I know what a hero is," the Chestnut answered. "A hero is a very brave man who is not afraid to risk his life in order to save others. Oh, I've heard about heroes before."

"Oh, have you? Then perhaps you can tell me if there are girl heroes as well as men heroes."

"I'm not sure," said the truthful Chestnut, "I never heard of one. But I know there are dog heroes, for you remember when we heard of the dog jumping into the water after the little girl, it was said that the people always called him 'Hero' after that."

"Yes, but I'm pretty sure the heroes are nearly all men," said wise Miss Maple. "There must have been lots of them in early Canada,

5   65

for the story says a band of heroes, and that means a whole lot. I hope it rains all through the story, it makes my leaves so cool."

And to please the Maple it really did rain, a soft gentle summer rain, which freshened the leaves of the dusty trees, and pattered softly on the window-pane, while all was quiet to hear the tale.

We may be quite sure that the rude and savage Indians often annoyed and troubled the white people, now settling in the little French towns of Montreal and Quebec. The Iroquois were the worst, of course, because they were the strongest and fiercest; and then, too, they thought the French people were against them.

One winter a great many of these war-like savages had gathered round Montreal and other places near. They had made up their minds to sweep down on the homes of the "pale-faces" as soon as they could get a chance.

The people in the towns were very much afraid, for these Indians were so strong and terrible that it would be easy for a large number of them to kill all the French people in Canada. So they had to try some way to keep them from getting into their towns and sounding the war-whoop in their ears.

The way was soon found. At Montreal a young soldier, Adam Daulac, a Frenchman, gathered a band of brave young fellows round him; all like himself, eager to meet the Indians and fight them.

The Governor gave them leave and they started out, seventeen young men going to meet perhaps hundreds of fighting Iroquois.

But the little band had brave hearts and strong spirits. Besides, were they not fighting for their homes and the country they held so dear?

Going on their way rather slowly, in canoes, for they were not so good at paddling the canoes as the Indians were, they came at last to the rapids of the Long Saut on the Ottawa River. And the brave young men never got any farther, for the fight between them and the Indians took place right there.

Close to the rapids, where the waters were roaring and tumbling over the rocks, they found a rude little fort.   It had at one time been built by a party of Indians, and it was neither very firm nor strong now.

But as they were tired out they were willing to wrap themselves up in their blankets, and wait here till the Indians came along.

And here they were soon joined by some forty friendly Indians led by a very brave chief, who begged that he and his Indians might have leave to join the Frenchmen in fighting the hated Iroquois.   Daulac and his men were well pleased to get their help.   They hoped, too, that these Indians would be able to show them the best way to fight with other Indians.

It was only two or three days after they had reached the Long Saut that Indian canoes were seen shooting the rapids.   Daulac's men shot at them as they neared the shore.   Some of the Indians were killed but some got away through the woods, and ran to tell the rest of the party about the Frenchmen and their plan.   The Iroquois were angry and surprised.   They were sure they could easily fight a handful of Frenchmen in a broken-down fort, so jumping

into their canoes they paddled quickly to the
rapids.

Daulac and his men at their morning meal
were surprised by the news that almost a
hundred canoes were on their way and could
even now be seen. Before they had time to get
ready, the Iroquois canoes reached the smooth
water at the foot of the rapids, and the Indians
leaped out to rush on the fort.

But the French drove them back and the
Indians lost quite a few men.

They then tried to get Daulac and his men to
give up the fort and their guns to them, but the
Frenchmen only laughed and told them to fight
for them.

The Iroquois hardly knew what to do. They
had thought it would be so easy to take the poor
Frenchmen and their rough little fort, and here
they were driving them back and laughing at
them.

So they fell back into the forest and began to
build a fort for themselves. The French, in the
meantime, set to work to make their fort a little
stronger.

But they had hardly finished their work when the savages again rushed at them, and the fight began in earnest. This time the Iroquois held blazing torches and tried to throw them into the fort. But the soldiers in the fort knew how to fire a gun, and they never stopped till one torch-bearer after another fell. And the fort was not yet taken.

On they came again, this time led by a brave Indian chief. A bullet from the fort struck their leader and he fell. One of the young Frenchmen ran out, cut off the dead chief's head, and set it up on one of the posts of the fort, right before the eyes of the Indians. The Indians were raging and again they made a dash on the fort, only to be driven back again. And now they began to feel that they could not hope to get the better of the plucky Frenchmen.

But not far away they knew where there were five hundred other Iroquois camping. A message was quickly sent to them, asking them to come to their help.

While they waited the Indians kept all the time annoying the French, trying to tire them out, so that they would not be able to stand against them and their five hundred friends when they came.

All this time the French were suffering greatly from hunger, thirst, cold and want of sleep. They had no water and did not dare to leave the fort for any, because the Iroquois were all along the river front. But they went to work and dug down into the ground till a little stream of muddy water was found.

To add to their troubles, all but four of the forty Indians who had joined them now left them and went over to the side of the Iroquois. Only twenty were now left to fight for Canada. Yet when the Iroquois called on them to give up, they would not—they would rather fight till death came.

At last the other Iroquois came, and then the Indians felt all was in their hands. How could twenty brave five hundred?

On they rushed on the fort, but it was only to be driven back time and again, and to see many of their brave fighters fall. Then the Indians held a council of war—to talk it all over and lay some plans to make the French give in.

The only way now, was to get in by a trick. So they cut down trees and made themselves each a shield by putting three or four logs together. Holding these in front of them, they came once more near to the fort. The trees formed a wooden wall, behind which the Indian was safe from French bullets. Closer and closer they came to the fort until with a wild whoop they threw their shields away and leaped upon the walls. Hatchets in hand, they cut and tore them all away, to get to the centre.

But the brave Frenchmen, what about them? All was lost they knew. But they had fought like heroes and they were bound to die like heroes. Knife and axe in hand they met the Indians, and when the middle of the fort was reached only four were still alive. Three of them were at once put to death, but the Indians kept the other to torture him.

All the brave band gave up their lives, but their wonderful courage saved their country. After the fight at the Long Saut, the Indians seemed to think better of their plans to destroy Montreal and Quebec.

If seventeen Frenchmen had been almost too much for a large band of Indians, how would they meet a whole town of such fighters?

So for a time Canada enjoyed a rest from the attacks of the savage Iroquois.

———————

BRAVE MADELEINE.

Madeleine de Verchères was a young French girl about fourteen years old. She lived not many miles from Montreal on the side of the broad St. Lawrence River. Her home was right in the path of the Iroquois as they made their trips to Montreal, and so was often troubled by the Indians. For this reason the house had been given the name of the Castle Dangerous of Canada.

One bright fall morning more than two hundred years ago, a little girl might have been seen standing on a small wharf by the river, looking up and down.

This was Madeleine. Her father and mother were both away and she was in full charge of the house. Just now she was out looking for a friend who was coming to help her pass some of the time she had to stay alone.

Suddenly as she stood there, she heard the sound of a gun. A man standing near her

shouted, " Run ! run ! the Iroquois !" and Madeleine turned to see some fifty of the hated
Indians not far off.

She did not need to be told again to run, but
swift as a deer sped to the house, the Indians
firing after her.

For safety in those days a fort was built near
the house and as soon as Madeleine was once
inside of it she cried to the men " To arms ! to
arms !" But the men were frightened to death,
and could do nothing. Then, brave little girl
as she was, Madeleine took charge. With her
own hands she helped the men to mend broken
places in the walls and make the fort strong.
For the Indians she knew were only waiting a
chance to get in the fort. They were afraid to
try, for they did not know how many soldiers
were in it. Madeleine's plan was to try to
make them believe that the fort was full of
soldiers. We will see, too, how well she carried
it out.

A long covered passage led from the fort to
the block-house, as it was called. This was a
strong wooden fort where the guns and powder

were kept. There were only two soldiers here and they, too, were much afraid. When Madeleine ran in one of them stood with a match in his hand ready to put it to the powder and blow them all up. This was to save them from the torture of the Iroquois.

But Madeleine faced him, and in anger knocked the match out of his hand, crying as she did so, "You are a miserable coward." She then sent the two soldiers to the fort, took a gun herself and then spoke to her two little brothers, Louis and Alexander, both younger than herself.

"We must fight," she said gravely, "Remember that our father has taught us to be brave. We are fighting for our king and our country." Then the three soldiers took their place in the fort with the others.

In that fort and house there were but two soldiers, a servant, an old man of eighty, two boys, and some women and children. For the Iroquois had fallen upon the men at work in the fields round about. There was no one to lead them but this little girl of fourteen. If the fifty Indians waiting round had only known this, they would have rushed in and made short work of them all.

But they were afraid, and so they watched and waited, hoping to get into the fort by some trick or plan.

Very soon a canoe was seen coming slowly near. In this canoe was Madeleine's visitor, a young French lady with her husband and family. Poor Madeleine was very much afraid that the Iroquois would see them, fall upon them, and kill them at once. None of the men would go to the river to warn them, so Madeleine by a little trick fooled the watching Indians, ran to the river, and by her courage soon got the whole family safely into the fort. And now she had some more frightened, helpless ones to care for.

For a whole week, they kept the Indians away. When any of them came near, they were fired at. Madeleine even had the only cannon in the fort fired off, and the wondering Indians waited, thinking the fort was indeed full of soldiers.

At night they could hear the cry, "All's well!" ring out from the fort to the block-house.

During all the week Madeleine hardly dared to stop watching to eat her meals, and she slept like a soldier indeed, with her head on her arms and her gun beside her.

Her two brothers, brave little lads as they were, did all they could to help her, and the two soldiers, though frightened at first, soon became a great help to their young leader.

The Indians did not quite see how it was done, but they found that if they went near, a gun went off close beside them. So they kept far enough away.

But help was near. Some of the men who had been working in the fields when the Indians came, had got away to Montreal. There they told of the Indians coming, and help was sent to Castle Dangerous. The two boys in the fort brought the great news to Madeleine. A French soldier and forty men were seen in canoes on the river.

Madeleine was glad enough to give up her place of leader to the brave captain whose coming was so welcome. The Iroquois did not wait long when they saw the French soldiers, but quickly made off.

The Governor at Montreal was told the whole story of Madeleine's bravery, and we may be sure that her father and mother soon came home to rejoice over the safety of their brave children.

And through the patter of the rain-drops, the Maple found time to whisper, "There were girl-heroes *then*; I think it is quite likely there are some yet."

THE ENGLISH AND THE FRENCH
AT WAR.

Now all these things we have been hearing about Canada, happened in the days when France owned Canada.

Since the days of Cartier, Canada had been in the hands of the French people. The people were nearly all French, the governors were sent from France, and the priests were there teaching the religion of France.

But England also had a place in the new world. The land lying south of Canada had by this time a large number of both English and Dutch people living in it.

For about a hundred years after the first white people came to live in the new world, the people in the two parts of the big country lived at peace with each other.

Both sides wanted to be friendly with the Indians, as the chief trade of the new country was in furs, which they got mostly from the

Indians. Now the Iroquois Indians were more friendly to the English people, while the Hurons and Algonquins stuck close to the French.

At first the English and the French let the Indians fight amongst themselves, and took no part in their wars.

But the Iroquois became more and more of a trouble to the French people as the towns began to grow. These wild red men, cunning and fierce, would sweep down like the wind on the French villages, burn them up, and go back to their homes, often with many French scalps hanging from their belts.

The French soon began to blame the English for these raids, and to say that they helped the Iroquois to annoy them in this way.

The Governor of Canada at this time was Frontenac, one of the best and bravest governors that Canada ever had. He made up his mind to punish the English for helping the Iroquois, and show them that France could hurt them too. The Indians were very fond of Frontenac and he always got along well with them. He used to go to visit them in their

6

camps, and would often ask the chiefs to come and have a feast with him. He made friends with the children and feasted the squaws, who used to amuse him in the evenings with their Indian dances. In this way he got them to like him, and very soon gathered a large band of friendly Indians round him.

They joined in with the French soldiers and together they marched upon three English towns when the people never dreamt of them coming. In a very cruel way they killed the people of these towns and destroyed and burned the towns altogether.

This made the English very angry, for they said they had done nothing to the French to make them act so mean and cruel. They did not feel afraid of the French as Frontenac thought they would, but were now most anxious to fight them. Then was begun the first real war between the English and the French in the New World.

Frontenac, the governor, was at Montreal when word was brought to him that the English fleet was planning to take Quebec. Thirty-two ships and a large number of soldiers had already left Boston on their way to Canada, hoping to surprise the French.

But an Indian, friendly to France, had heard of the plan, and had come a long way to tell the governor all about it.

As soon as Frontenac heard that his much loved town was to be attacked, he made haste to get there, anxious to reach it by land before the English got there by water. He was gladly welcomed back by his people, who felt safe when they saw their old gray-haired soldier–leader once more at their head.

He quickly set every one to work to make the fort so strong that the English would have some hard work to do before Quebec was theirs. So well did they do their work, that when the English ships sailed in on the St. Lawrence, they found a carefully guarded town waiting for them.

And more than that, they had a leader to fight who was bold and brave as a lion. For Frontenac was not going to give up the town he had worked so hard to keep together. He had kept it from the attacks of the brutal Iroquois, and was not going to give it up, just because the English asked for it. No, he would give up his own life first—and his brave spirit put courage into the hearts of his soldiers.

To help him, a large band of men had come to Quebec from all the different parts of Canada. And the old governor looked on his army with pride and joy. Such fine soldiers! Strong, active, young Frenchmen, and sturdy Indians who never were so happy as when fighting. With these behind him, he need not fear to meet the English.

The leader of the English ships sent one of his men with a message to Frontenac as soon as the boats reached Quebec.

This English soldier was blind-folded, and led by a round-about way up the heights, so that he might find out nothing about the town.

Then when taken before the governor and his soldiers, who were all dressed up in their bright, shining uniforms, he was much surprised by the show.

But he gave his message to the governor, and asked for an answer within an hour.

"An answer!" shouted the angry old governor. "Tell your leader he will get my answer from the mouths of my cannon. Let him do his best and I will do mine."

There was nothing now to be done but fight. The English were brave and plucky, but try as hard as they could, they seemed to be firing at a solid rock, and hurting no one. While their own boats in the open river got all the shots from the French guns.

One of the first shots carried away the flag from the English leader's own ship. A brave young Canadian leaped out of a canoe, and swimming out on the river while English bullets were whizzing round his ears, brought the flag to shore amidst the cheers of his comrades. This flag was hung in the great church at Quebec, where it stayed for many years to tell of the time the Canadians had driven their foe away.

Still the fight went on. Frontenac was sending a fiery answer right into the English ships.

But it seemed to the English that they could hear nothing but the echo of their own guns striking the solid rock and falling away harmless. The leader felt it was useless to keep up the fight. His food was nearly gone now. If they waited long, the St. Lawrence would be frozen hard, and they could not pass through. They hardly wanted to stay in front of Quebec all winter in the hands of the French. So as they could not hope to take Quebec, the English leader quietly took his ships, and sailed away, leaving the victory to Frontenac and the French. When the people of Quebec saw that the English had really gone they nearly went wild with joy. Cheer after cheer sent the echoes from the rocks now, instead of the sound of guns.

A big procession was formed. At the head of the procession they carried the flag taken from the English. All day long the noise was kept up, the people cheering and shouting the name of their hero Frontenac.

At night a big bon-fire was lit on the top of the rock, its merry blaze keeping the night light as day.

For the Canadians felt justly proud that they had been able to keep their land from passing out of their hands into the hands of the strangers who had no claim upon it.

ACADIA AND ITS SAD STORY.

In the early days, the place we now call Nova Scotia was known by the name of Acadia. It was then, as now, a beautiful place, its fields were rich and green, its skies were blue and sunny. There were many pretty bays, winding rivers and shady valleys. Its people were mostly farmers, quiet, busy, happy people.

In the days of Champlain, a little town had been started there and named Port Royal. This town was taken by the English just before they tried to take Quebec from the French, and England's flag now waved over Acadia.

But the people of Acadia were French. They liked the French rule and the French people. And they did not like the English. They were always hoping the French would win their land back again, and so would not obey the English governors who were sent to them.

When any English people came to settle in Acadia, the Acadian farmers did them all the harm they could. They set fire to their houses and barns, and then watched with delight the flames shooting up to the sky. Their priests, too, led them on to hate and hurt the English, as they too were hoping to fall once more under French rule.

The English soon saw that there would be no peace in the land, and no real English rule there as long as the Acadians were so true to the French. So the people of Acadia were given their choice, either to say they would be true to England and fight for her, or else to leave the country altogether within a year.

Leave their country! The farmers would not think of it. Be true to England! They did not want to be that either.

So they stayed on, thinking they were safe. The English surely did not mean to put them out. But England did mean it, and we will see how she did it too.

It was the lovely warm month of August. In the land round the beautiful Minas river, every-thing still held the glow of summer upon it. In the valley the grain stood yellow, waiting for the harvest. The cattle on the hillsides ate the sweet, green grass and looked quietly round with content in their eyes. The people were busy in the rich fields and gardens gathering in their heavy crop.

Everything was calm and quiet until one day the news came to the surprised village—an English soldier and three hundred men had landed on the shore of their river.

"What does he want?" the people asked each other eagerly—but no one knew.

As the days passed on and the soldiers did them no harm, their fear seemed to pass away.

The work of the village went on as usual. The barns were filled, the cattle looked after, the fruit gathered. On Sunday they walked to their little church, and at nights they met in each other's homes for friendly talk.

Some of them had even begun to say that the soldiers would pass the winter with them in their quiet homes.

But the English soldier and his men were only waiting a chance to do their work. For they had been sent to drive these poor people from the land they loved so well.

When the harvest was nearly over, a message was sent through the village. All men old and young, and all boys ten years of age and over were ordered to meet in the church on a Friday afternoon at three o'clock, to hear what the English leader had to say to them.

The farmers did not know what to make of such an order. But they made haste to get all their work done by Thursday night, so as to have time for their holiday on Friday.

The church was full on Friday afternoon and strangely quiet when the English leader, as kindly as he could, told them his awful news.

By order of the King of England the Acadians were to be sent from the country. They would be taken away in English ships. They could take their money and as much of their goods as the ships would hold without loading them down.

But all else was to be left. Cosy homes, rich fields, full barns, cattle—all was to be left behind, while the people who had worked so hard to get them must be taken far away.

There was wild weeping in that village when the news was spread. In that church the men were to be kept prisoners till the English ships came to carry all away.

At different times a few men were let out to visit their wives and children, who could do nothing to help them but only wait round and weep at their hard lot.

At last, when October frosts had begun to colour their loved hillsides with red and golden hues, the English ships arrived. The work of getting all on board began. The people then began really to feel that all was too true—that they must pack up their goods, march on the English ships, and leave their homes forever.

It was a sad sight. Even the English soldiers felt it, and did their hard duty as kindly as they could.

Mothers and children got on the ships weeping and mourning. The weak and the old ones were carried carefully, by sad, kind friends, all alike broken-hearted at leaving their homes.

The English leader was good to them. He tried to put all near friends on the same ship.

The soldiers did not treat them badly, nor hurt their goods. But they made them leave their homes and watched carefully that no one should get away.

The last ship sailed away before Christmas, and the village was left empty. The houses, barns, mills and church were set on fire and the only living creatures to be seen were the cattle, still grazing on the quiet hills alone.

From other parts of Acadia, the people were driven out in much the same way, and found homes in many different spots.

Some came back very soon after, but many of them never saw their early home again.

THE ENGLISH TAKE QUEBEC.

The first fight which took place in Canada between the English and the French was not the last one by any means. The two peoples never stopped fighting for many years, after that first battle.

The English had been getting the better of France, too. They had taken some of their strongest forts. But the prize they wished for was Quebec. If they could take that rock-bound fort, all Canada would be open to them.

In the Old Land, France and England were at war. It was not strange, then, that their children in the New, were eager to fight also.

A brave soldier, General Montcalm, was sent from France to take charge of Quebec and the soldiers there. He was a well trained, wise leader, and under him the city and the country seemed quite safe.

But against the French general the English

soldiers proudly set their hero, General James Wolfe, whose name will ever cling to Canada.

General Wolfe was a very young man to be the leader of a large army. But he had been in the English army since he was fifteen years old, and by his wisdom and bravery had worked right up to the top. He was not a very fine-looking man, and he was not very strong of body either, for he was often sick. But he was so wise and gentle, so kindly and true, and brave, that all his soldiers loved him. They were ready to go anywhere with him or do anything for him.

With an English leader full of courage bound to take Quebec, and a brave French general to take care that the English did not get in, it was hard to tell who would win in the end.

The English were full of hope, trusting to their wise general and well trained soldiers. The French, in turn, laughed at the thought of any-one taking their rocky mountain fort. It was not so very many years since they had quickly sent the English from their shores.

Montcalm at Quebec made every place strong.

Every way into the city was closed except one, and that was to let their own soldiers in from the river front.

Big black cannon stood on the hills, pointing down on the river. All along the river front were big ships loaded with guns, while fire-ships and fire-rafts floated on the river in front of the city. There seemed no place for the English to make their way into the city.

At last the English ships sailed up the river, and the French tried their first plan. This was to destroy all the English ships, at once, with their fire-ships. The fire-ships were loaded with pitch, tar, fire-works, and other things which catch fire easily. These boats were sent out on the river right into the middle of the English ships. Then they were set on fire, and the French thought the whole line of ships would burn up.

But the English soldiers and sailors stood watching as one after another of the fire-ships took fire and blazed up till the whole river was in flames. The noise and the flames were dreadful. But the English sailors were not afraid.

They rowed out in boats to the burning ships, towed them out of harm's way or ran them ashore. And the great plan of the governor to burn up English boats failed at the very start.

The English tried many ways to get into the city. Montcalm, in his strong place in the town, looked on and smiled at the different plans of the English. As long as he could keep Wolfe and his soldiers out of the city all was well. Once they got in things might be different.

Wolfe was very anxious to meet the French on the field of battle, for he was sure his soldiers could face them—but no way was open. If he could but find a way to climb the steep hill and reach the broad plains on the top, where each might fight fairly!

But the summer passed away and little had been done. Many of the soldiers were sick and unfit to fight. Worst of all, Wolfe himself took sick and lay ill with a fever for many days in a farm house. The English were very down-cast.

But if the French still held Quebec, they were in a bad way, too, though the English did not know it.

7

There was sickness among their soldiers, too; food was scarce, and the town was almost in ruins from the attacks of the English soldiers. Montcalm hardly knew how his city could stand the biting cold of a Canadian winter.

But Wolfe was better again. The soldiers gathered their courage for one last trial. The young general, pale and worn, stood with glass in hand, carefully looking over the heights. His keen eye hit upon one spot where it seemed easy to get up. This spot is now known as Wolfe's Cove. From this cove a little crooked path led to the top. Up this path he would send a few men to guard the top till the whole army could follow.

Who would go? Twenty-four soldiers offered themselves at once to be the first to climb the steep side of the cliff. On a dark night they were rowed to the spot, Wolfe himself being in one of the first boats. In deep silence they reached the shore. The French soldiers, in the darkness, took them for Frenchmen coming with supplies. In a few minutes the brave twenty-four had taken prisoners the soldiers guarding the cove, and were at the top, the rest quickly following. It was hard work to climb that steep hill, hanging on to the rough bushes that grew on the sides, but the young general was one of the first to reach the top. At last he stood with his army on the grassy plains, facing the city of Quebec, ready to fight and win, or die.

When the day broke, Montcalm heard the startling news: "The English army is on the heights!" Quickly he ordered his soldiers round him, and galloped to the Plains of Abraham, where the English were. On his big black horse the French leader rode up and down, waving his sword and calling his men to fight for the glory of France.

At ten o'clock in the morning the two armies met. The French soldiers in their white uniforms, and the Indians and French traders in their odd dress, faced the scarlet-coated Englishmen, and the Highlanders in their kilts.

The French fired on the red lines of men which faced them, but the English waited for their leader's word.

Riding at their head Wolfe gave the order.

With wild cheers the English red-coats rushed on the French. The lines broke, and the French fell in heaps around them. The English still pressed on, and soon drove them before them to the city. The battle of the Plains of Abraham was won in a few minutes.

Montcalm was shot through the body, but lived till he reached the city he had tried so hard to save.

The brave Wolfe was shot three times. The third time he fell, never to rise again. Loving arms carried him to a quiet spot. Only once did he speak, and that was when he heard the cry, "They run! they run!"

"Who run?" he asked, trying to rise.

"The French!" was the glad answer.

With a happy smile the General turned on his side. "Now God be praised, I die in peace." The brave voice was silent, and the lion heart had stopped beating. Wolfe, the hero, had given up his life for his country.

The little spot where he fell is still green. A stone there tells the simple story—"Here Wolfe died victorious."

His body was taken to England. It lies still in Westminster Abbey among England's good and great ones.

All England wept over her brave soldier, and in a little English village Wolfe's mother wept for her true son who had died so nobly.

Down in Quebec stands a splendid monument on which the names of the two great soldiers, Montcalm and Wolfe, are joined together. Canadians were proud to raise that stone to the two great men who gave their lives up, fighting for Canada.

But with the battle of the Plains of Abraham, France lost Canada. From that time the Union Jack has floated over Canada's fair land. English and French now joined hand in hand to make the new land great.

"I think the holidays are near," said the Chestnut tree to the Maple.

"Why?" the Maple asked.

"Well, you see, it is getting very warm. My blossoms have gone long ago."

"Is that why you think the holidays are

near? It has been warm for weeks now, and school is still open."

The poor Maple felt badly just then. Some boy who had not been thinking of the harm he might do, had swung on a branch of hers, until it broke.

It was a big, beautiful branch, too, hanging heavy with leaves. No wonder the Maple carried a sad heart under her thick, green leaves. She could not tell of her trouble to anyone but the Chestnut, and that good tree had been trying to think of some way to make her forget about it. But it was hard work to talk to a cross tree.

However, she did not feel much hurt.

"Oh, no!" she said brightly. "That is not why I think the holidays are near. I have heard the children talk about it. They are all going away to the country, and to the lakes, and other fine places."

"And we stay here and see nothing," said the Maple.

"Why, now, Maple, you know trees never want to go away. I'm sure I should hate to leave the school-yard."

"But we will not hear any more stories for two whole months," said the Maple, who was bound to be miserable just then.

"I'm sorry for that," whispered the Chestnut. "I never knew so many things had happened before. I didn't know people liked to fight each other. We never see them do it now."

"Oh, they stopped all that when the English took Canada. They made the Indians do right, I'm sure. I wish we could hear some more about the Indians, though. Perhaps we'll have another story yet."

"Let's look in and listen now," said the Chestnut, bending over. And, as they peeped in, what was their delight to hear the name of the new story.

PONTIAC AND HIS INDIANS FIGHT THE ENGLISH.

The English were now the rulers of the New World, but the Indians were not at all pleased with the change.

They did not like the English as well as they did the French.

The English had not had as much to do with the Indians as the French had, and they did not know so well how to treat them. They stopped giving them the little presents of hatchets, beads, and other things, which the French always had ready for their Indian friends.

For a long time, too, the French had given the Indians guns and powder, as well as clothes. And now the English would give them none of these things, and the Indians felt themselves ill-used.

Then the English fur traders were not like the French traders. They were often very cruel to the Indians, cheating them and treating their women and children very unkindly.

When the French soldiers and their officers were at the forts, the Indians used to come in to see them, lounge round, look at everything, and make themselves very much at home in their simple, easy way. But the English soldiers would not let them stay round the forts. They thought they were a great bother, and used to order them roughly away, sometimes touching them with their guns to make them move faster. The Indians felt this to be a great insult.

And all through the country great bands of white people were going to take up land. Wherever they went the Indians had to get out and go deeper into the forests to be by themselves. And the thinking Indians saw that the white man would soon own the whole land, and there would be no place for the red man at all.

All these things made them uneasy and unhappy. As they had always liked the French, they were quite ready to blame the English for all their troubles.

The French did not like the English either, and they helped to make the Indians feel worse towards the English.

They told the Indians that their "Great Father," the King of France, had been sleeping when the English crept in and stole Canada. But he was awake now, and his great armies were even now on the way to save his red children from the hands of the English.

From all this sprang a great Indian war, which lasted for nearly three years after the English took Canada.

The great mover in this war was Pontiac, a very noted Indian chief of the Algonquin Indians. He was a man of great power among the Indian tribes.

At this time he was about fifty years old. He was very brave and strong, could speak well and plan well, and was very cunning and wise.

When his mighty voice was heard calling the chiefs of the tribes to a great meeting, they all gathered quickly round him.

From village to village, and from camp to camp, the messengers went with the signs of war. These were a black and purple war belt made of wampum, and a tomahawk stained red.

In every case the chiefs took the belt and picked up the hatchet. By this they showed themselves ready for war.

Their plan was to go to all the forts where the English soldiers were, destroy the forts, kill the soldiers, and drive all the English out of the land.

Pontiac himself lived with his own tribe on an island in the Detroit river. From his cabin of bark and rushes he could look across at Fort Detroit, where the English soldiers were. He picked on this fort as the first one he and his brother Indians should take.

One bright May morning, he and his savages marched into the fort ready to take it and all within it. But an Indian girl had told the English officer all about Pontiac's plan. So, when the bold Indians went into the fort, they found everywhere plenty of armed soldiers to receive them.

The Indian chief was greatly vexed and annoyed to see that his plan must fail. But with great cunning he said to the officers that he was much surprised to see so many soldiers ready with their guns. "For," he said, "we have only come to smoke the peace-pipe with our English brothers whom we love."

But the "English brothers" knew he did not love them, though he said he did, and they watched him pretty closely.

In a few days he was joined by other bands of fierce Indians, and together they made an attack on Fort Detroit. For a long time (several months) the war lasted, but, at last, the Indians were driven back and beaten by the English.

But at other forts, the Indians did more harm and mischief than at Fort Detroit.

Close to the edge of the deep blue waters of Lake Huron, stood Fort Michillimackinac, the strongest fort in that part of the country. Near to it is the island of Mackinac, called so by the Indians, who thought it was shaped like a turtle. For their name for the fort meant in Indian "The Great Turtle."

In the early days the Jesuit priests had started a mission there. At Fort Michillimackinac there was now a mission house, a fort, and a cluster of Canadian houses. It was also a great centre for the fur trade. There were many tribes of Indians living round the fort, and they were all willing to join Pontiac in his war. They were just waiting their chance to seize the fort and the soldiers there.

When the news was brought that Pontiac had started to take Fort Detroit, they could wait no longer. All the tribes gathered themselves together and made ready to take Fort Michillimackinac.

Early one fine day in June the soldiers were enjoying a holiday. Outside of the fort two tribes of Indians were playing a game of ball. The soldiers stood round, near the gates, watching the friendly game.

Everything looked peaceful and pleasant. The gates of the fort were wide open. The captain and his men were careless and happy, without sword or guns near them. The Indian chiefs moved around, too, enjoying themselves, while any number of Indian squaws stood quietly near, wrapped in their coarse blankets.

The Indians in the game were leaping and jumping in the grass, yelling and screaming as they chased the ball.

Suddenly a shot sent the ball flying near to

the gates of the fort.   Rushing after it went the
screaming band of savages.   Before the soldiers
had time to act, the cries were changed into the
fierce Indian war-whoop.   The squaws handed
out the hatchets which they had under their
blankets.   The Indians leaped on the soldiers,
cutting and scalping without mercy.   The officers
were led away prisoners, and Fort Michillimackinac was in the hands of the Indians.

It did not take them long to clear the place,
and the cry soon arose, "All is finished."   The
Indians stayed there for a few days drinking and
feasting in the empty fort.   Then they began to
feel afraid of what they had done, and fearful of
what the English would do to them when they
found it out.   So they ran away, but not before
the fort was cleared, and not an English soldier
was to be found around there.

But the Indians did not gain anything by their
fight with the English.   In a few years the
English had quite got the better of them.
Pontiac died, and the Indian tribes went back
to their hunting and fishing in the forests and
lakes.   The red man's land had become the
home of the white man.

THE HERO OF QUEENSTON HEIGHTS.

On the grassy slopes of the heights which run along the Niagara river, near the little town of Queenston, there stands a fine monument.

Many Canadian boys and girls have climbed the steep hill to look upon the tall stone which Canada was pleased to put there in honour of her hero, Major-General Brock. This brave soldier, who was killed at Queenston while fighting for Canada, left a name behind him which will always be dear to the sons and daughters of the fair Dominion.

In the New World the English settlers had fought with their mother-land across the seas. And now, next door to Canada was born a new country, the United States of America.

But the people there were not satisfied even to be free and to own their land. Canada was a big, rich country lying very near to them. Why should they not have her, too, and drive Old England's flag from the New World !

So to gain Canada, another war was begun. For three years the Americans tried hard to take Canada, and make it part of their country. But at last they had to give up, since Canada fought so hard to remain true to England.

Early in the war the battle of Queenston Heights was fought. The Canadians won the battle, but at great cost, for there she lost her loved leader, Brock.

Niagara River stretches along for some way between Canada and the United States. Standing on the heights at Queenston, we can look across the blue waters of the river, partly ours and partly our neighbours'. We can see the people on the other side in their houses, their factories, and their streets.

On the morning of October 13, eighty-six years ago, the trees in the gorge and on the slopes of the heights must have looked very beautiful.

The early frosts would just have touched the thick growth of leaves, and scarlet maples, yellow beeches, and crimson oaks would be mixed with the dark green pines and firs.

But there was no time then to look on the bright colours of the leaves, or to watch the pale morning sun shining on the quiet water of the river.

Instead, soldiers were running to and fro on the banks, eagerly watching the river. For boats were seen, filled with American soldiers, crossing from the other side to Canada.

The Canadians on the heights gave these soldiers a warm enough welcome from the mouth of the cannon placed on the cliff. But the Americans were in charge of a brave soldier, who urged his men on, until in a short time, a strong body of soldiers were on the Canadian side, ready for battle.

General Brock was not at Queenston, but at Fort George some miles away. He had risen before daylight, and hearing the noise of cannon knew at once that the Americans were making an attack on Queenston.

On his horse he galloped at full speed to the battle. Day was just breaking, and he saw the heights filled with American soldiers. Straight up the hill Brock rode at the head of his men, cheering them on with his hearty words, "Follow me, boys!" But one of the enemy, picking out

8

the brave General from amongst his men, shot at him and he fell, shot through the breast.

With a cry the men behind him sped on, anxious to get at the enemy who had killed their loved leader. Brock only lived long enough to ask that his death be kept from the rest of the soldiers. While the battle went on, the General lay in a house at Queenston, cold and still in death.

The Americans were driven right to the brow of the hill, and were in a place of great danger. Behind them was the foaming Niagara River, before them the angry Canadians, who were twice as fierce now without a leader as they had been with one.

And now more soldiers and a new leader came for the Canadians, and once more they dashed on the enemy. The Americans had lost a number of their men and could not stand against the sudden storm of bullets rained on them by the Canadians. Their brave leader fell. Amidst the shouts of the soldiers and the yells of the savage Indians in the Canadian army, they fled to the edge of the steep. Numbers threw themselves over the cliff, some swam across the river, and some got away in boats.

The American leader sent in a flag of truce, and the battle of Queenston Heights was won.

Besides the monument standing on Queenston Heights, there is another stone in memory of Brock in St. Paul's Cathedral, London, England. There lies the great soldier's sword and helmet. On one side of the stone is carved a scene showing the General dying in the arms of an English soldier. An Indian standing sadly by, shows the deep love that the red man had for the brave English soldier.

In these days a whizzing electric car carries you quickly round the heights to the bottom of the hill. There we may see a big square stone. Many years ago the Prince of Wales, on a visit to Canada, placed that great stone there to mark the spot where Brock fell in battle.

The war went on for three years, and the names of Stoney Creek, Beaver Dam, Lundy's Lane and other places now point to spots where battles were fought in that war.

All Canada joined hands to fight bravely and well. Young men and old men, and even the women and girls helped—taking their share of work at home when the men were called away to fight.

But one woman, Laura Secord, did more than stay at home. She did a very brave act, for which her name is remembered to-day and placed amongst the brave ones of Canada.

She was the wife of a soldier living at Queenston. This soldier had been hurt in the battle of Queenston Heights.

At Beaver Dams, near to where the city of St. Catharines stands now, there was an English officer with a few soldiers and a few Indians. Secord heard that the Americans were going to attack this place. He was too ill to go himself to tell the English, but his wife offered to go for him.

Early in the morning, she started off for her long walk of twenty miles. Her way led through thick woods, where she had to pick her way carefully for fear of snakes or animals, and also keep out of the way of American soldiers.

It took her all day to reach her stopping-place. Here she first came across a band of Indians, who scared her by their yells and fierce cries.

But she was soon taken to the officer in charge and gave him her news. He made such good use of his time that when the Americans came to *take*, they had instead, to *give up* to the English.

TECUMSEH.

It was during this war, too, that we find the name of another great Indian chief, Tecumseh. This time, though, the Indian is fighting on the side of the English; not against them, like Pontiac.

Tecumseh was a fine Indian and a great fighter. His name in Indian meant "a tiger crouching for his prey." He did not think the Americans had treated him well, and was only too glad to join the English to fight against them.

When Brock called a meeting of the Indians and asked them to help him in his fight, Tecumseh made a great speech.

He told Brock that all the Indians were ready to give their last drop of blood, fighting for their "great father," the English King.

Tecumseh had great power over the other Indians. He kept them back when they would have been too wild and fierce.

The Indian chief felt very sad at the death of Brock, but he kept right on fighting with the English. He was killed in one of the battles of the war. He and his braves were in the swamp, not far from a river, when the Americans came upon them. The rest of the English soldiers had run away, but the Indians stayed and fought the Americans.

The American leader shot Tecumseh just as the red man had his tomahawk raised to strike him.

The soldiers treated the red man's dead body very badly, though he had died a brave death, fighting for the people and the country he loved.

Amongst his people are to be found still very many who love the English. For Canada, after all, has been very kind to the red man, whose land she took.

The two trees still stand side by side, whispering to each other.

The school is quiet now and the windows are closed.

They feel very lonely and quiet without the children. They have very little to talk about and there is nothing at all to listen to.

But often in the cool evenings we may see their branches twined together. If we could listen to them, perhaps we should hear the Maple telling the Chestnut some of her Grandfather Maple's stories.

For we may be sure that half of the stories that might be told of Canada's early days, were not heard in the school-room.

www.ingramcontent.com/pod-product-compliance
Lightning Source LLC
Chambersburg PA
CBHW022138020726
47496CB00008B/2459